The Tale of
Brownie Beaver

Arthur Scott Bailey

Contents

THE TALE OF
BROWNIE BEAVER

BY

Arthur Scott Bailey

I
A QUEER PLACE TO LIVE

The village near one end of Pleasant Valley where Farmer Green often went to sell butter and eggs was not the only village to be seen from Blue Mountain. There was another which Farmer Green seldom visited, because it lay beyond the mountain and was a long distance from his house. Though he owned the land where it stood, those that lived there thought they had every right to stay there as long as they pleased, without being disturbed.

It was in this village that Brownie Beaver and his neighbors lived. It was a different sort of town, too, from the one where Farmer Green went each week. Over beyond Blue Mountain all the houses were built in a pond. And all their doors were under water. But nobody minded that because--like Brownie Beaver--everybody that dwelt there was a fine swimmer.

Years and years before Brownie's time his forefathers had come there, and finding that there were many trees in the neighborhood with the sort of bark they liked to eat--such as poplars, willows and box elders--they had decided that it was a good place to live. There was a small stream, too, which was really the beginning of Swift River. And by damming it those old settlers made a pond in which they could build their houses.

They had ideas of their own as to what a house should be like--and very good ideas they were--though you, perhaps, might not care for them at all. They wanted their houses to be surrounded by water, because they thought they were safer when built in that manner. And they always insisted that a door leading into a house should be far beneath the surface of the water, for they believed that that made a house safer too.

To you such an idea may seem very strange. But if you were chased by an enemy you might be glad to be able to swim under water, down to the bottom of a pond, and slip inside a door which led to a winding hall, which in its turn led upwards into your house.

Of course, your enemy might be able to swim as well as you. But maybe he would think twice--or even three times--before he went prowling through your crooked hall. For if you had enormous, strong, sharp teeth--with which you could gnaw right through a tree--he would not care to have you seize him as he poked his head around a corner in a dark passage of a strange house.

It was in a house of that kind that Brownie Beaver lived. And he built it himself, because he said he would rather have a neat, new house than one of the big, old dwellings that had been built many years before, when his great-great-grandfather had helped throw the dam across the stream.

The dam was there still. It was so old that trees were growing on it. And there was an odd thing about it: it was never finished. Though Brownie Beaver was a young chap, he worked on the dam sometimes, like all his neighbors. You see, the villagers kept making the dam wider. And since it was built of sticks and mud, the water sometimes washed bits of it away: so it had to be kept in repair.

If Brownie Beaver and his friends had neglected their dam, they would have waked up some day and found that their pond was empty; and without any water to hide their doorways they would have been safe no longer.

They would have had no place, either, to store their winter's food. For they were in the habit of cutting down trees and saving the bark and branches too, in order to have plenty to eat when cold weather came and the ice closed their pond.

Some of their food they carried into their houses through a straight hall which was made for that very purpose. And some of the branches they fastened under water, near the dam. It was just like putting green things into a refrigerator, so they will keep.

Now you see why Brownie Beaver would no more have thought of building his house on dry land than you would think of building one in a pond. Everybody likes his own way best. And it never once occurred to Brownie Beaver that his way was the least bit strange.

Perhaps it was because his family had always lived in that fashion.

II
HOW TO FELL A TREE

Brownie Beaver could do many things that other forest-people (except his own relations) were not able to do at all. For instance, cutting down a tree was something that nobody but one of the Beaver family would think of attempting. But as for Brownie Beaver--if he ever saw a tree that he wanted to cut down he set to work at once, without even going home to get any tools. And the reason for that was that he always had his tools with him. For strange as it may seem, he used his teeth to do all his wood-cutting.

The first thing to be done when you set out to fell a tree with your teeth is to strip off the bark around the bottom of the trunk, so that a white band encircles it. At least, that was the way Brownie Beaver always began. And no doubt he knew what he was about.

After he had removed the band of bark Brownie began to gnaw away chips of wood, where the white showed. And as he gnawed, he slowly sidled round and round the tree, until at last only the heart of the tree was left to keep the tree from toppling over.

Then Brownie Beaver would stop his gnawing and look all about, to pick out a place where he wanted the tree to fall. And as soon as Brownie had made up his mind about that, he quickly gnawed a few more chips out of the heart of the tree on the side toward the spot where he intended it to come toppling down upon the ground.

Brownie Beaver would not have to gnaw long before the tree would begin to lean. All the time it leaned more and more. And the further over it sagged, the faster it tipped. Luckily, Brownie Beaver always knew just the right moment to jump out of the way before the tree fell.

If you had ever seen him you might have thought he was frightened, because he never failed to run away and hide as the tree crashed down with a sound almost like thunder.

But Brownie was not at all frightened. He was merely careful. Knowing what a loud noise the falling tree would make, and that it might lead a man (or some other enemy) to come prowling around, to see what had happened, Brownie used to stay hidden until he felt quite sure that no one was going to trouble him.

You can understand that waiting, as he did, was no easy matter when you stop to remember that one of Brownie's reasons for cutting down a tree was that he wanted to eat the tender bark to be found in the tree-top. It was exactly like knowing your dinner was on the table, all ready for you, and having to hide in some dark corner for half an hour, before going into the dining-room. You know how hungry you would get, if you had to do that.

Well, Brownie Beaver used to get just as hungry as any little boy or girl. How he did tear at the bark, when he finally began to eat! And how full he stuffed his mouth! And how he did enjoy his meal! But everybody will admit that he had a right to enjoy his dinner, for he certainly worked hard enough to get it.

III
STICKS AND MUD

Like the dam that held back the water to form the pond where Brownie Beaver lived, Brownie's house was made of sticks and mud. He cut the sticks himself, from trees that grew near the bank of the pond; and after dragging and pushing them to the water's edge he swam with them, without much trouble, to the center of the pond, where he wished to build his house. Of course, the sticks floated in the water; so Brownie found that part of his work to be quite easy.

He had chosen that spot in the center of the pond because there was something a good deal like an island there--only it did not rise quite out of the water. A good, firm place on which to set his house-- Brownie Beaver considered it.

While he was building his house Brownie gathered his winter's food at the same time. Anyone might think he would have found it difficult to do two things at once like that. But while he was cutting sticks to build his new house it was no great trouble to peel the bark off them. The bark, you know, was what Brownie Beaver always ate. And when he cut sticks for his house there was only one thing about which he had to be careful; he had to be particular to use only certain kinds of wood. Poplar, cottonwood, or willow; birch, elm, box elder or aspen-- those were the trees which bore bark that he liked. But if he had cut down a hickory or an ash or an oak tree he wouldn't have been able to get any food from them at all because the bark was not the sort he cared for. That was lucky, in a way, because the wood of those trees was very hard and Brownie would have had much more work cutting them down.

A good many of Brownie Beaver's neighbors thought he was foolish to go to the trouble of building a new house, when there were old ones to be had. And there was a lazy fellow called Tired Tim who laughed openly at Brownie.

"When you're older you'll know better than to work like that," Tired Tim told him. "Why don't you do the way I did?" he asked. "I dug a tunnel in the bank of the pond; and it's a good enough house for anybody. It's much easier than building a house of sticks and mud."

But Brownie told Tired Tim that he didn't care to live in a hole in the bank.

"Nobody but a very lazy person would be willing to have a house like that," Brownie said.

Tired Tim only laughed all the harder.

"Old Grandaddy Beaver has been talking to you," he remarked. "I saw him taking you over to the dam day before yesterday and telling you where to work on it. Of course, that's all right if you're willing to work for the whole village. But I say, let others do the work! As for me, I've never put a single stick nor a single armful of mud on that dam; and what's more, I never intend to, either.

"My tunnel in the bank suits me very well. Of course, it may not be so airy in summer as a house such as you're making for yourself. But I don't live in my house in summer. So what's the difference to me? In summer I go up the stream, or down- -just as it suits me--and I see something of the world and have a fine time. There's nothing like travel, you know, to broaden one," said Tired Tim.

Brownie Beaver stopped just a moment and looked at the lazy fellow. He was certainly broad enough, Brownie thought. He was so fat that his sides stuck far out. But it was no wonder--for he never did any work.

"You'd better take my advice," Tired Tim told Brownie.

But Brownie Beaver had returned to his wood-cutting. He didn't even stop to answer. To him, working was just fun. And building a fine house was as good as any game.

IV
THE FRESHET

The rain had fallen steadily for two days and two nights-not just a gentle drizzle, but a heavy downpour.

For some time it did not in the least disturb Brownie Beaver and his neighbors--that is to say, all but one of them. For there was a very old gentleman in the village known as Grandaddy Beaver who began to worry almost as soon as it began to rain.

"We're a-going to have a freshet," he said to everybody he met. "I've seen 'em start many a time and I can always tell a freshet almost as soon as I see it coming."

Grandaddy Beaver's friends paid no heed to his warning. And some of them were so unkind as to laugh when the old gentleman crawled on top of his house and began to mend it.

"You young folks can poke fun at me if you want to," said Grandaddy Beaver, "but I'm a-going right ahead and make my house as strong as I can. For when the freshet gets here I don't want my home washed away."

All day long people would stop to watch the old fellow at work upon his roof. And everybody thought it was a great joke--until the second day came and everybody noticed that it was raining just as hard as ever.

But no one except Grandaddy Beaver had ever heard of a freshet at that time of year. So even then nobody else went to work on his house, though some people *did* stop smiling. A freshet, you know, is a serious thing.

As the second day passed, the rain seemed to fall harder. And still Grandaddy Beaver kept putting new sticks on the roof of his house and plastering mud over them. And at last Brownie Beaver began to think that perhaps the old gentleman was right, after all, and that maybe everybody else was wrong.

So Brownie went home and set to work. And all his neighbors at once began to smile at him.

But Brownie Beaver didn't mind that.

"My roof needed mending, anyhow," he said. "And if we **should** have a freshet. I'll be ready for it. And if we don't have one, there'll be no harm done."

Now, all this time the water had been rising slowly. But that was no more than everyone expected, since it was raining so hard. But when the second night came, the water began to rise very fast. It rose so quickly that several families found their bedroom floors under water almost before they knew it.

Then old Grandaddy Beaver went through the village and stopped at every door.

"What do you think about it now?" he asked. "Is it a freshet or isn't it?"

In the houses where the water had climbed above the bedroom floors the people all agreed that it was a freshet and that Grandaddy Beaver had been right all the time. But there were still plenty of people who thought the old gentleman was mistaken.

"The water won't come any higher," they said. "It never has, at this time of year." But they looked a bit worried, in spite of what they said.

"It's a-going to be the worst freshet that's happened since you were born," their caller croaked. "You mark my words!"

When he came to Brownie Beaver's house Grandaddy found that there was one person, at least, that had taken his advice.

"I see you're all ready for the freshet!" the old gentleman remarked. "They laughed at me; but I was right," he said.

"They laughed at me, too," Brownie Beaver told him.

"There's nobody in this village that'll laugh again tonight," Grandaddy said very solemnly, "for there's a-going to be a flood before morning."

V

BROWNIE SAVES THE DAM

B rownie Beaver was always glad that he had taken Grandaddy's advice about the freshet. And Brownie's neighbors were glad that he had, too. For that was really the only thing that saved the village from being carried away by the flood of water that swept down upon the pond, after it had rained for two days and two nights.

The pond rose so quickly and the water rushed past so fast that people had to scramble out of their houses and begin working on them, to keep them from being washed away.

That rush of water meant only one thing. The pond was full and running over! And just as likely as not the dam would be carried away--the dam on which Grandaddy Beaver had worked when he was a youngster, and on which his own grandaddy had worked before him. It would take years and years to build another such dam as that.

Now, with almost everybody working on his own house, there was almost no one left to work upon the dam. But people never stopped to think about that. They never once remembered that out of the whole village old Grandaddy and Brownie Beaver were the only persons whose houses had been made ready for the freshet and that those two were the only people with nothing to do at home.

"There'll be plenty to help save the dam," everybody said to himself. "I'll just work on my house."

Now, Brownie Beaver knew that there was nothing more he could do to make his house safe, so he swam over to the dam, expecting to find a good many of his neighbors there. But old Grandaddy Beaver was the only other person he found. And he seemed worried.

"It's a great pity!" he said to Brownie. "Here's this fine dam, which has taken so many years to build, and it's a-going to be washed away-- you mark my words!"

"What makes you think that?" asked Brownie.

"There's nobody here to do anything," said Grandaddy Beaver. "The spillways of this dam ought to be made as big as possible, to let the freshet pass through. But I can't do it, for I can't swim as well as I could once."

Brownie Beaver looked at the rushing water which poured over the top of the dam in a hundred places and was already carrying off mud and sticks, eating the dam away before his very eyes.

"I'll save the dam!" he cried. "You?" Grandaddy Beaver exclaimed. "Why, what do you think you can do?" Being so old, he couldn't help believing that other people were too young to do difficult things.

"Watch me and I'll show you!" Brownie Beaver told him. And without saying another word he swam to the nearest spillway and began making it bigger.

Sometimes he had to fight the freshet madly, to keep from being swept over the dam himself. Sometimes, too, as he stood on the dam it crumbled beneath him and he found himself swimming again.

How many narrow escapes he had that day Brownie Beaver could never remember. When they happened, he didn't have time to count them, he was working so busily. And if old Grandaddy Beaver hadn't told everyone afterward, how Brownie saved the great dam from being swept away, and how hard he had worked, and how he had swum fearlessly into the torrent, people wouldn't have known anything about it.

To be sure, they had noticed that the water went down almost as suddenly as it rose. But they hadn't stopped to think that there must have been some reason for that. And when they learned that Brownie Beaver was the reason, the whole village gave him a vote of thanks.

They wanted to give him a gold-headed cane, too. But they were unable to find one anywhere.

When Brownie Beaver heard of that he said it was just as well, because he seldom walked far on land and there wasn't much use in a person's carrying a cane when he swam, anyhow. Although it was sometimes done, he had always considered it a silly practice--and one that he would not care to follow.

VI
A HAPPY THOUGHT

Brownie Beaver liked to know what was going on in the world. But living far from Pleasant Valley as he did, he seldom heard any news before it was quite old.

"I wish--" he said to Mr. Crow one day, when that old gentleman was making him a visit--"I wish someone would start a newspaper in this neighborhood."

Mr. Crow told Brownie that he would be glad to bring him an old newspaper whenever he happened to find one. "Thank you!" Brownie Beaver said. "You're very kind. But an old newspaper would be of no use to me."

"Why not?" Mr. Crow inquired. "They make very good beds, I've been told. And I suppose that is what you want one for."

"Not at all!" Brownie replied. "I'd like to know what's happening over in Pleasant Valley. It takes so long for news to reach us here in our pond that it's often hardly worth listening to when we hear it--it's so old. Now, what I'd really prefer is a newspaper that would tell me everything that's going to happen a week later."

Mr. Crow said he never heard of a newspaper like that.

"Well, somebody ought to start one," Brownie Beaver answered.

Mr. Crow thought deeply for some minutes without saying a word. And at last He cried suddenly:

"I have an idea!"

"Have you?" Brownie Beaver exclaimed. "What is it, Mr. Crow?"

"I'll be your newspaper!" Mr. Crow told him.

At that Brownie Beaver looked somewhat doubtful.

"That's very kind of you," he said. "But I'm afraid it wouldn't do me much good. You're so black that the ink wouldn't show on you at all--- unless," he added, "they use *white* ink to print on you."

"You don't understand," old Mr. Crow said. "What I mean is this: I'll fly over here once a week and tell you everything that's happened. Of course," he continued, "I can't very well tell you everything that is going to take place the following week. But I'll do my best."

Brownie Beaver was delighted. And when Mr. Crow asked him what day he wanted his newspaper Brownie said that Saturday afternoon would be a good time.

"That's the last day of the week," Brownie Beaver remarked, "so you ought to have plenty of news for me. You know, if you came the first day of the week there would be very little to tell."

"That's so!" said Mr. Crow. "Well say 'Saturday,' then. And you shall have your newspaper without fail--unless," he explained--"unless there should be a bad storm, or unless I should be ill. And, of course, if Farmer Green should want me to help him in his cornfield, I wouldn't be able to come. There might be other things, too, to keep me at home, which I can't think of just now," said Mr. Crow.

Again Brownie Beaver looked a bit doubtful.

"I hope you'll try to be regular," he told Mr. Crow. "When a person takes a newspaper he doesn't like to be disappointed, you know."

Old Mr. Crow said that he hoped nothing would prevent his coming to Brownie's house every Saturday afternoon.

"There's only one more thing I can think of," he croaked, "that would make it impossible for me to be here. And that is if I should lose count of the days of the week or have to see a baseball game or fly south for the winter."

"But that's *three* things, instead of only *one*," Brownie Beaver objected.

"Well--maybe it is," Mr. Crow replied--"the way you count. But I call it only one because I said it all in one breath, without a single pause."

"I hope you won't tell me the news as fast as that," said Brownie Beaver, "for if you did I should never be able to remember one-half of it."

But Mr. Crow promised that he would talk very slowly.

"You'll be perfectly satisfied," he told Brownie. "And now I must go home at once, to begin gathering news."

VII
A NEWFANGLED NEWSPAPER

After Mr. Crow flew back to Pleasant Valley to gather news for him, Brownie Beaver carefully counted each day that passed. Since Mr. Crow had agreed to be his newspaper, and come each Saturday afternoon to tell him everything that had happened during the week, Brownie was in a great hurry for Saturday to arrive.

In order to make no mistake, he put aside a stick in which he gnawed a notch each day. And in that way he knew exactly when Saturday came.

That was probably the longest day in Brownie Beaver's life. At least, it seemed so to him. Whenever he saw a bird soaring above the tree-tops he couldn't help hoping it was Mr. Crow. And whenever he heard a *caw*--caw far off in the distance Brownie Beaver dropped whatever he happened to be doing, expecting that Mr. Crow would flap into sight at any moment.

Brownie had many disappointments. But Mr. Crow really came at last. He lighted right on top of Brownie Beaver's house and called "Paper!" down the chimney--just like that!

Brownie happened to be inside his house. And in a wonderfully short time his head appeared above the water and he soon crawled up beside Mr. Crow.

"Well, I *am* glad to see you!" he told Mr. Crow.

"Peter Mink caught a monstrous eel in the duck pond on Monday," Mr. Crow said. Being a newspaper, he thought he ought to say nothing except what was news--not even "Good afternoon!"

"Mr. Rabbit, of Pine Ridge, with his wife and fourteen children, is visiting his brother, Mr. Jeremiah Rabbit. Mrs. Jeremiah Rabbit says she does not know when her husband's relations are going home," Mr. Crow continued to relate in a singsong voice.

"Goodness gracious!" Brownie Beaver exclaimed.

"Fatty Coon--" Mr. Crow said--"Fatty Coon was confined to his house by illness Tuesday night. He ate too many dried apples."

"Well, well!" Brownie Beaver murmured. And he started to ask Mr. Crow a question. But Mr. Crow interrupted him with more news.

"Mrs. Bear had a birthday on Wednesday. An enjoyable time was had by all--except the pig."

"Pig?" Brownie Beaver asked. "What pig?"

"The pig they ate," said Mr. Crow. And he went right on talking. "On Thursday Mr. Woodchuck went to visit his cousins in the West. Mrs. Woodchuck is worried."

"What's she worried about?" Brownie inquired.

"She's afraid he's coming back again," Mr. Crow explained.

"I *have* heard he was lazy," Brownie said. "What happened on Friday?"

"Tommy Fox made a visit. But he didn't have a good time at all," Mr. Crow reported, "and he left faster than he came."

Brownie Beaver wanted to know where Tommy Fox made his visit.

"At Farmer Green's hen-house," Mr. Crow explained.

"Why did he hurry away?" Brownie asked.

"Old dog Spot chased him," Mr. Crow replied. "But you mustn't ask questions," he complained. "You can't ask questions of a newspaper, you know."

"Well--what happened on Saturday?"

"There you go again!" cried Mr. Crow. "Another question! I declare, I don't believe you ever took a newspaper before--did you?"

Brownie Beaver admitted that he never had.

"Then--" said Mr. Crow--"then don't interrupt me again, please! I'll tell you all the news I've brought. And when I've finished I'll stop being a newspaper and be myself for a while. And then we can talk. But not before!" he insisted.

Brownie Beaver nodded his head. He was afraid that if he said another word Mr. Crow would grow angry and fly away without telling him any more news.

"On Saturday--this morning, to be exact"--said Mr. Crow, "there came near being a bad accident. Jimmy Rabbit almost cut off Frisky Squirrel's tail."

Mr. Crow paused and looked at Brownie Beaver out of the corner of his eye. He knew that Brownie would want to know what prevented the accident. But he was in no hurry to tell him.

For a few moments Brownie waited to hear the rest. But a few moments was more than he could endure.

"Why didn't Jimmy cut off his tail?" Brownie asked eagerly.

"There!" said Mr. Crow. "You've done just as I told you not to. So I shall not tell you the rest until next Saturday.... You see, you have a few things to learn about taking a newspaper." And 'he would give Brownie no more news that day. To be sure, he was willing to talk--but only about things that had happened where Brownie Beaver lived.

VIII
MR. CROW IS UPSET

Brownie Beaver couldn't help feeling that Mr. Crow had not treated him very well, because Mr. Crow hadn't told him all the news about Frisky Squirrel's tail. He thought that maybe there were things about a newspaper that even Mr. Crow didn't know.

Another week had passed. Brownie knew that it had, because since Mr. Crow's last call he had cut a notch in a stick each day. And there were now seven of them.

Late Saturday afternoon Mr. Crow came back again. He lighted on top of Brownie's house and called "Paper!" down the chimney, just as he had a week before.

Brownie Beaver came swimming up once more.

"Look here!" he said to Mr. Crow. "I don't believe yon know much about being a newspaper, do you?"

That surprised Mr. Crow.

"What do you mean?" he asked.

"A newspaper--" said Brownie Beaver--"a newspaper is always left on, a person's doorstep. I've talked with a good many people and not one of them ever heard of a paper being left on the roof."

Mr. Crow's face seemed to grow blacker than ever, he was so angry.

"How can anybody leave a newspaper on your doorstep, when the step's under water?" he growled.

Brownie Beaver did not answer that question, for he had something else to say to Mr. Crow.

"I've talked with a good many people," he said once more, "and not one of them ever heard of such rudeness as **shouting down a person's chimney**. If there was anybody asleep in the house, it would certainly wake him; and if a person had a fire in his house, shouting down the chimney might put it out."

Mr. Crow looked rather foolish.

"I'll try to think of some way of leaving your newspaper that will suit us both," he said. Then he **hemmed** and began to tell Brownie the week's news.

"On Sunday," said Mr. Crow, "there was a freshet."

"I knew that before you did," said Brownie Beaver.

Mr. Crow looked disappointed.

"How?" he asked.

"Why, I live further up the river than you," said Brownie Beaver. "And since freshets always come **down** a river, this one didn't reach you till after it had passed me."

Something made Mr. Crow peevish.

"I don't believe you'd care to hear any more of my news," he said. "You appear to know it already. Perhaps you'll be kind enough to tell me the sort of news you prefer to hear."

"Certainly!" Brownie Beaver replied. "Now, there's the weather! I've talked with a good many people and they all say that a good newspaper ought to tell the weather for the next day."

Mr. Crow cocked an eye up at the sky.

"To-morrow will be fair," he said.

"I'm told that a good newspaper ought to tell a few jokes," Brownie Beaver continued.

But Mr. Crow sneered openly at that. "I'm a **newspaper**--not a **jest-book**," he announced.

"Then you refuse to tell any jokes, do you?" Brownie Beaver asked him.

"I certainly do!" Mr. Crow cried indignantly.

"Very well!" Brownie said. "I see I'll have to take some other newspaper, though I must say I hate to change--after taking this one so long."

"I hope you'll find one to suit you," Mr. Crow said in a cross voice. And he flew away without another word. He was terribly upset. You see, he had enjoyed being a newspaper, because it gave him an excuse for asking people the most inquisitive questions. He had intended all that week to ask Aunt Polly Woodchuck whether she wore a wig. But he hadn't been able to find her at home. And now it was too late--for Mr. Crow was a newspaper no longer.

As for Brownie Beaver, he succeeded in getting Jasper Jay to be his newspaper. Though Jasper told him many jokes, Brownie found that he could not depend upon Jasper's news. And as a matter of fact, Jasper made up most of it himself. He claimed that the ***newest news*** was the best.

"That's why I invent it myself, right on the spot," he explained.

IX
THE SIGN ON THE TREE

On one of Brownie Beaver's long excursions down the stream he came upon a tree to which a sign was nailed. Now, Brownie had never learned to read. But he had heard that Uncle Jerry Chuck could tell what a sign said. So Brownie asked a pleasant young fellow named Frisky Squirrel if he would mind asking Uncle Jerry to come over to Swift River on a matter of important business.

When Uncle Jerry Chuck appeared, Brownie Beaver said he was glad to see him and that Uncle Jerry was looking very well.

"I've sent for you," said Brownie, "because I wanted you to see this sign. I can tell by the tracks under the tree that the sign was put up only to-day. And I thought you ought to know about it at once, Uncle Jerry."

As soon as he heard that, Uncle Jerry Chuck stepped close to the tree and began to read the sign.

Now, there was something about Uncle Jerry's reading that Brownie Beaver had heard. People had told him that Uncle Jerry Chuck couldn't tell what a sign said unless he read it *aloud*. That was why Brownie Beaver had sent for him, for Brownie knew Uncle Jerry well enough to guess that if anybody *asked* Uncle Jerry to read the sign, Uncle Jerry would insist on being paid for his trouble.

But now Uncle Jerry was going to read the sign for himself. And Brownie Beaver moved up beside him, to hear what he said.

The sign looked like this:

NO HUNTING
OR FISHING
ALOUD

Uncle Jerry repeated the words in a sing-song tone.

"I don't think much of that," he said. "It's bad enough to be hunted by people who make a noise, though you have *some* chance of getting away then. But if they can't make a noise it will be much more dangerous for all of us forest-people."

If Tommy Fox hadn't happened to come along just then Uncle Jerry wouldn't have found out his mistake. But Tommy Fox soon set him right. As soon as he had talked a bit with Uncle Jerry he said:

"What the sign really means is that no hunting or fishing will be permitted. That last word should be 'allowed,' instead of 'aloud.' It's spelled wrong," he explained.

"That's better!" Uncle Jerry cried. "Now there'll be no more hunting in the neighborhood and we'll all be quite safe.... Farmer Green is kinder than I supposed."

When Brownie Beaver heard that, he said good-by and started home at once to tell the good news to all his friends. He had leaped into the river and was swimming up-stream rapidly when Uncle Jerry called to him to stop.

"There's something I want to say," Uncle Jerry shouted. "I think you ought to pay me for reading the sign."

But Brownie Beaver shook his head.

"I didn't ask you to read the sign for me," he declared. "You read it for *yourself*, Uncle Jerry. And besides, you didn't know what it meant until Tommy Fox came along and told you.... If you want to know what I think, I'll tell you. I think you ought to pay Tommy Fox something."

Uncle Jerry at once began to look worried. He said nothing more, but plunged out of sight into some bushes, as if he were afraid Tommy Fox might come back and find him.

X
A HOLIDAY

There was great rejoicing in the little village in the pond when Brownie Beaver returned with the good news that there would be no more hunting and fishing. And when old Grandaddy Beaver said that everybody ought to take a holiday to celebrate the occasion, all the villagers said it was a fine idea.

So they stopped working, for once, and began to plan the celebration. They thought that there ought to be swimming races and tree-felling contests. And Brownie Beaver said that after the holiday was over he would suggest that someone be chosen to go down and thank Farmer Green for putting the notice on the tree.

The whole village agreed to Brownie's proposal and they voted to see who should be sent. Brownie Beaver himself passed his hat around to take up the votes. And it was quickly found that every vote was for Brownie Beaver. He had even voted for himself. But no one seemed to care about that.

Then the swimming races began. There was a race under water, a race with heads out of water--and another in which each person who took part had to stay beneath the surface as long as he could.

That last race caused some trouble. A young scamp called Slippery Sam won it. And many people thought that he had swum up inside his house, where he could get air, without being seen. But no one could prove it; so he won the race, just the same.

Next came the tree-felling contest. There were six, including Brownie Beaver, that took part in it. Grandaddy Beaver had picked out six trees of exactly the same size. Each person in the contest had to try to bring his tree to the ground first. And that caused some trouble, too, because some claimed that their trees were of harder wood than others--and more difficult to gnaw--while others complained that the bark of their trees tasted very bitter, and of course that made their task unpleasant.

Those six trees, falling one after another, made such a racket that old Mr. Crow heard the noise miles away and flew over to see what was happening.

After everybody crept out of his hiding-place some time afterward (everyone had to hide for a while, you know), there was Mr. Crow sitting upon one of the fallen trees.

"What's going on?" he inquired. "You're not going to cut down the whole forest, I hope."

Then they told him about the celebration. And Mr. Crow began to laugh.

"What are you going to do next?" he asked.

"We're a-going to send Brownie Beaver over to Pleasant Valley to thank Farmer Green for his kindness in putting an end to hunting and fishing," said old Grandaddy Beaver. "And he's a-going to start right away."

Mr. Crow looked around. And there was Brownie Beaver, with a lunch-basket in his hand, all ready to begin his long journey.

"Say good-by to him then," said Mr. Crow, "for you'll never see him again."

"What do you mean?" Grandaddy Beaver asked. And as for Brownie--he was so frightened that he dropped his basket right in the water.

"I mean----" said Mr. Crow--"I mean that it's a very dangerous errand. You don't seem to have understood that sign. In the first place, it was not Farmer Green, but his son Johnnie, who nailed It to the tree."

"Ah!" Brownie Beaver cried. "That is why one of the words was misspelled!"

"No doubt!" Mr. Crow remarked. As a matter of fact, not being able to read he hadn't known about the word that was spelled wrong. "In the second place," he continued, "the sign doesn't mean that hunting and fishing are to be stopped. It means that no one but Johnnie Green is going to hunt and fish in this neighborhood. He wants all the hunting and fishing for himself. That's why he put up that sign. And instead of hunting and fishing being stopped, I should say that they were going to begin to be more dangerous than ever.... They tell me," he added, "that Johnnie Green had a new gun on this birthday."

Brownie Beaver said at once that he was not going on the errand of thanks.

"I resign," he said, "and anyone that wants to go in my place is welcome to do so."

But nobody cared to go. And the whole village seemed greatly disappointed, until Grandaddy Beaver made a short speech.

"We've all had a good holiday, anyhow," he said. "And I should say that was something to be thankful for."

XI
BAD NEWS

Have you heard the news?" Tired Tim asked Brownie Beaver one day. "There's going to be a cyclone."

"A cyclone?" Brownie exclaimed. "What's that? I never heard of one."

"It's a big storm, with a terrible wind," Tired Tim explained. "The wind will blow so hard that it will snap off big trees."

"Good!" Brownie Beaver cried. "Then I won't have to cut down any more trees in order to reach the tender bark that grows in their tops."

Tired Tim laughed. "You won't think it's very 'good,'" he said, "when the cyclone strikes the village."

"Why not?" Brownie inquired.

"Because--" said Tired Tim--"because the wind will blow every house away. It will snatch up the sticks of which the houses are built and carry them over the top of Blue Mountain. Then I guess you'll wish you had taken my advice and not built that new house of yours.

"I shall be safe enough," the lazy rascal continued. "All I'll have to do will be to crawl inside my house in the bank; for the wind can't very well blow the ground away."

Brownie Beaver thought that Tired Tim was just trying to scare him.

"I don't believe there's going to be any such thing!" he exclaimed.

"Don't you?" Tim grinned. "You just go and ask Grandaddy Beaver. He's the one that says there's going to be a cyclone."

At that Brownie Beaver stopped working and hurried off to find old Grandaddy Beaver. And to his great dismay, Grandaddy said that what Tired Tim had told him was the truth.

"It's a-coming!" Grandaddy Beaver declared. "I saw one once before in these parts, years before anybody else in this village was born. And when I see a cyclone a-coming I can generally tell it a long way off."

"When is it going to get here?" Brownie asked in a quavering voice.

"Next Tuesday!" Grandaddy replied.

"What makes you think it's coming?"

"Well--everything looks just the way it did before the last cyclone," Grandaddy Beaver explained, as he took a mouthful of willow bark. "The moon looks just the same and the sun looks just the same. I had a twinge of rheumatics in my left shoulder yesterday; and to-day the pain's in my right. It was exactly that way before the last cyclone."

Brownie Beaver did not doubt that the old gentleman knew what he was talking about. He remembered that Grandaddy Beaver had warned everyone there was going to be a freshet. And though people had laughed at the old chap, the freshet had come.

Sadly worried, Brownie went and called on all his neighbors and asked them what they were going to do. And to his surprise he found that they were laughing at Grandaddy once more. They seemed to have forgotten about the freshet.

But Brownie Beaver could not forget that dreadful night. And now he tried to think of some way to keep his new house from being blown away by the great wind, which Grandaddy Beaver said was coming on Tuesday without fail.

XII
GRANDADDY BEAVER THINKS

It was on a Friday that Brownie Beaver first heard the cyclone was coming. And after making sure that Grandaddy Beaver knew what he was talking about when he said the great wind would sweep down upon the village on the following Tuesday, Brownie spent a good deal of time wondering what he had better do.

He wanted to save his house from being blown over the top of Blue Mountain. And he wanted to save himself from being carried along at the same time.

Before Friday was gone Brownie Beaver began to heap more mud and sticks upon his house, to make it stronger. And when Tired Tim came swimming past the lazy scamp laughed harder than ever.

"I see you're afraid of the cyclone," he called. "But what you're doing won't help you any. The wind will blow away those sticks easily enough.... What you ought to do is to dig a house like mine in the bank. Then you won't have to worry about any cyclone."

So Brownie set to work and made him a house like Tired Tim's. On Monday he had finished it. But he didn't like his new home at all.

"It's no better than a rat's hole," he said. "My family have never lived in such a place and I'm not used to it. I prefer my house that's built of sticks and mud. And I'm going to see if there isn't some way I can make it safe."

So Brownie went to Grandaddy Beaver again and asked him what he ought to do.

The old gentleman said he would try to think of a plan to save Brownie's house.

"I wish you would hurry," Brownie urged him. "To-day is Monday; and to-morrow the cyclone will be here.... What are you going to do to your own house, Grandaddy?"

"My house----" said Grandaddy Beaver--"my house is very old. It has had mud and sticks piled upon it every season for over a hundred years. You can see for yourself that it's much bigger than yours. And I reckon it's strong enough to stay where it is, no matter how hard the wind blows. But your house is different.... Let me think a minute!" the old gentleman said.

Brownie waited in silence while the old gentleman thought, with his eyes shut tight. Brownie watched him for a long time. Once or twice he thought he heard something that sounded like a snore. But he knew it couldn't be that--it was only the thoughts trying to get inside Grandaddy's head.

At last Grandaddy sat up with a start.

"Have you thought of something?" Brownie inquired.

"What's that?" Grandaddy asked. "Oh, yes! I've a good idea," he said. "What you must do is to tie your house so the wind can't blow it away."

Brownie thanked him. And he went away feeling quite happy again--until he reached home and started to follow Grandaddy's advice. Then he saw that he had forgotten something. He hadn't anything with which to tie his house and make it safe from the cyclone.

XIII
A LUCKY FIND

Brownie Beaver almost wished he hadn't spent so much time waiting for Grandaddy to tell him to tie down his house so it wouldn't be carried away by the big wind on the following day. With no rope--or anything else--to tie the house with, Brownie could not see that Grandaddy's advice was of any use to him.

Anyhow, he was glad he had done as Tired Tim had suggested and dug a house in the bank, where he could hide until the storm passed. But he felt sad at the thought of losing his comfortable home. And since he could hardly bear to look at it and imagine how dreadful it would be to have it blown over the top of Blue Mountain into Pleasant Valley, Brownie went for a stroll through the woods to try to forget his trouble.

He found himself at last in a clearing, where loggers had been at work. They had chopped down many trees. And the sight made Brownie Beaver angry.

"This is an outrage!" he cried aloud. "I'd like to know who has been stealing our trees. I suppose it's Farmer Green; for they say he's always up to such tricks." He took a good look around. And then he turned to go back to the village and tell what he had discovered.

Just as he turned he tripped on something. And something clinked beneath his feet. It didn't sound like a stone. So Brownie Beaver looked down to see what was there.

Now, in his anger he had quite forgotten the great storm. But as he saw what had tripped him he remembered it again. But he was no longer worried.

"Hurrah!" Brownie cried. "Here's just what I need!" And then he hurried back home again--but not to tell about the trees that had been stolen. He hastened home to ***chain down his house*** and save it from the great wind. For Brownie Beaver had found a chain, which the loggers had used to haul the logs out of the woods, and had forgotten.

It was almost dark when Brownie reached his house in the village in the pond. He was never a very good walker. And dragging that heavy chain behind him through the forest only made him slower than ever. Sometimes the chain caught on a bush and tripped him. But Brownie was so pleased with his find that he only laughed whenever he fell, for he was not hurt.

The whole village gathered round his house to watch him while he tied the chain on it and anchored the ends of the chain to the bottom of the pond with a big stone.

"Why do you do that?" people asked.

"He's afraid of the cyclone to-morrow," Tired Tim piped up, without waiting for Brownie to answer. "You know, old Grandaddy Beaver says that there's going to be a great wind. This young feller----" said Tim--"he's already dug a house in the bank near mine--ha! ha! He thinks Grandaddy knows. But I say that Grandaddy Beaver is a--a fine, noble, old gentleman," Tired Tim stammered. He had happened to glance around while he was talking; and to his surprise there was Grandaddy floating in the water close behind him.

"He certainly is," everybody agreed. "But we hope he's mistaken about the great wind."

When Tuesday came--which was the very next day--Brownie Beaver crept into his tunnel in the bank at sunrise. And he never came outside again until the sun had set.

When he saw that his house was still there, in the middle of the pond, he shouted with joy.

"Hurrah!" he cried. "The chain saved my house!" Then he noticed that all the other houses were still there, too. "How's this?" he asked Tired Tim, who stood on the bank beside him. "Did my chain save the whole village?"

Tired Tim grinned--for he was not too lazy to do that.

"There wasn't any cyclone," he said. "There wasn't a breath of wind all day. And old Grandaddy Beaver is so upset that he's gone to bed and won't talk with anybody."

XIV
WAS IT A GUN?

Everybody in the village where Brownie Beaver lived was very much upset. Most people were angry, too. And no doubt it was natural that they should feel that way, because while they were taking their midday naps a man had come and paddled about their village in a boat.

Brownie Beaver was the first to hear him and he quickly spread the alarm. There was a great scurrying as all the villagers stole out of their houses and swam away under water to hide in holes in the bank of the pond and in other places they knew.

Toward night, when they all came back again, the man had gone. But Brownie and his neighbors were still angry. You must remember that their rest had been disturbed and they were feeling somewhat sleepy.

So far as they could see, the man had done no damage either to their houses or to the dam. But people felt a bit uneasy just the same, until old Grandaddy Beaver looked all around and reported that the man had set no traps. You see, Grandaddy knew a great deal about traps. He had been caught in one when he was young. Luckily, he managed to get away; and he learned a few things that he never forgot.

Now, Brownie Beaver had begun to cut down a tree the night before. Something had interrupted him and he had left the tree not quite gnawed through and needing only a few more bites to bring it down. He was intending to finish his task soon after dark--which was the time he liked best for working.

Accordingly, after Brownie had finished his supper and had called at every house in the village to talk over the visit of the strange man, he swam to the shore of the pond and made his way to the slanting tree, which stood a short distance from the water.

It was quite dark. And that was what Brownie liked, because he could work without being disturbed--at least, that was what he thought.

Since he could see quite well in spite of the dark he had no trouble in finding his tree. And he lost no time in setting to work on it again.

He began to gnaw at it once more. But he hadn't moved more than half-way around the tree-trunk when something happened that almost frightened him out of his skin.

Right out of the darkness came a blinding flash of light. And at the same time a queer *click* sounded in the bushes close by.

Just for a moment Brownie Beaver was stiff with fear. But when the darkness closed in upon him again he ran for his life toward the pond. And plunging into the water he swam quickly to the bottom and hurried up his winding hall into his bedroom, where he crouched trembling upon his bed, wondering whether he had been shot.

Brownie knew that at night a gun made a flash of light. But this gun (if it was a gun) made no roar such as was made by the guns Brownie had sometimes heard at a distance in the woods. He wished that old Grandaddy Beaver was there. For he did not doubt that the old gentleman could tell him exactly what had happened.

XV
JASPER JAY'S STORY

After the blinding flash of light and the queer click had sent Brownie Beaver hurrying home from his partly gnawed tree, he stayed in his house for a long time before he ventured out again.

Indeed, the night was half gone when he at last he stole forth to find Grandaddy Beaver and tell him about his awful fright.

Brownie found the old gentleman resting after several hours' work upon the big dam. And when young Brownie told Grandaddy what had happened, the old gentleman didn't know just what to think.

"It couldn't have been a moonbeam," he said, "because there's no moon tonight. And I don't see how it could have been a gun, because there was no roar.... Did you hear a sort of whistle?" he asked. "Anything that sounded like a bullet passing over your head?"

Brownie Beaver shuddered at the mere mention of a bullet.

"I heard nothing but that odd click," he replied.

"That's what a gun sounds like when it's cocked," said Grandaddy Beaver. "But with a gun, the click comes first, the flash next, and the roar last of all. And here you tell me the flash came first, the click next, and there was no roar at all.... What's a body a-going to think, I'd like to know? It wasn't a gun--that's sure. And if you want to know what I say about it, why--I say that it was a very strange thing that happened to you. And I'd keep away from that tree for a long time."

"I had made up my mind that I'd do that," Brownie told him. And then he went home again. But he never went to sleep until almost noon the following day; for whenever he closed his eyes he seemed to see that blinding flash of light again.

When Jasper Jay came on Saturday afternoon to tell Brownie Beaver what had happened in the world during the past week he had an astounding piece of news.

"Here's something about you," Jasper told Brownie, as soon as he could catch his breath. Jasper had flown faster than usual that day, because he had such interesting news. "Your picture," he told Brownie, "is in the photographer's window, way over in the town where Farmer Green goes sometimes."

Brownie Beaver gave Jasper a quick look.

"I've often suspected," he said, "that you don't always tell me the truth. And now I know it. I've never been to the photographer's in my life. So how could he have my picture, I should like to know?"

"But you don't have to go to the photographer's to have your picture taken," Jasper Jay retorted. "Why couldn't the photographer come to you?"

"I suppose he could," Brownie Beaver said. "But he's never been here."

Jasper Jay gave one of his loud laughs.

"That--" he said--"that is just where you are mistaken. And when I explain how I came by this news, maybe you'll believe me.

"Tommy Fox told it to me," Jasper went on, "and old dog Spot told it to him. Everybody knows that old Spot sometimes goes to town with his master. They were there yesterday. And Spot saw your picture himself. What's more, he heard the photographer tell Farmer Green that he came up here almost a week ago, hid his camera in some bushes, and set a flashlight near a half--gnawed tree. And when you started to work on the tree that night you brushed against a wire, and the flashlight flared up, and the camera took your picture before you could jump away.... Now what do you say?" Jasper Jay demanded. "Now do you think I'm telling you the truth?"

Brownie Beaver was so surprised that it was several minutes before he could speak. Then he said:

"Grandaddy Beaver was right. It wasn't a gun. I was just having my picture taken." Brownie was actually pleased, because he knew he was the only person in his village that had ever had such a thing happen to him.

After that he was ready to believe everything Jasper Jay told him. So Jasper related some wonderful news. And it would hardly be fair for anyone not present at the time to say that it wasn't perfectly true-- every word of it.

XVI
LOOKING PLEASANT

After Jasper Jay left Brownie Beaver, on that day when Jasper told Brownie that the photographer had made a flashlight picture of him, Brownie could hardly wait for it to grow dark. He had made up his mind that he would go back to that same tree, which was still not quite gnawed through; and he hoped that he would succeed in having his picture taken again. Like many other people, Brownie Beaver felt that he could not have too much of a good thing.

There was another reason, too, for his going back to the tree. If the light flared again and the click sounded in the bushes, Brownie intended to go right into the thicket and get his picture before anybody else could carry it away with him. (You can understand how little he understood about taking photographs.)

Well, the dark found Brownie back at the tree once more. And he began once more to gnaw at it. He tried to look pleasant, too, because he had heard that that was the way one should look when having his picture taken.

He found it rather difficult, gnawing chips out of the tree and smiling at the same time. But he was an earnest youngster and he did the best he could.

Brownie Beaver kept wishing the flashlight would go off, because--what with smiling and gnawing--his face began to ache. But no glare of light broke through the darkness.

It was not long before Brownie had gnawed away so many chips that the tree began to nod its head further and further toward the ground. And Brownie wished that the flash-light would hurry and go off before the tree fell.

But there was not even the faintest flicker of light. It was most annoying. And Brownie was so disappointed that for once he forgot to be careful when he was cutting down a tree. He kept his eyes on the bushes all the time, instead of on the tree--as he should have done. And all the time the tree leaned more and more.

At last there was a *snap!* Brownie Beaver should have known what that meant. But he was so eager to have his picture taken that he mistook the *snap* for the *click* that he had first heard almost a week before.

He thought it must be the click of a camera hidden in the bushes. And he stood very still and looked extremely pleasant. Now, Brownie Beaver should have known better. But like most people, for once he made a mistake. What he really heard was the tree snapping. And before he could jump out of the way the tree came crashing down upon him and pinned him fast to the ground. He saw a flash of light, to be sure, and a good many stars. But all that only came from the knock on his head which the tree gave him.

XVII
BROWNIE ESCAPES

When the tree crashed down upon Brownie Beaver and held him fast, it was some time before he came to his senses. Then he did not know, at first, where he was nor what had happened to him. But at last he remembered that he had been cutting down a tree not far from the pond and he saw that it must have fallen upon him.

Of course, the first thing that occurred to him was to call for help. But just as he opened his mouth to shout, another thought came into his head. ***Perhaps some man might hear him--or a bear!*** And Brownie Beaver closed his mouth as quickly as he had opened it.

Then he tried to squirm from under the tree-trunk. But he couldn't move himself at all. Next he tried to push the tree away from him. But he couldn't move the tree either.

For a long while Brownie Beaver struggled, first at one impossible thing, and then at the other. And all the time the tree seemed to grow heavier and heavier.

Finally, Brownie stopped trying to get free and began to feel hungry.

You can see that he must have been worried, because there was the tree, with plenty of bark on it which he could eat. But he never noticed it for a long time.

At last, however, he happened to remember that in the beginning he had started to cut down that very tree so he could reach the bark and eat it.

Then Brownie Beaver had a good meal. And just as he finished eating, another thought came into his head. ***Why shouldn't he gnaw right through the tree?***

Since there seemed to be no answer to that question, he began to gnaw big chips out of the wood. And in a surprisingly short time he had cut the tree apart just where it pressed upon him.

Then, of course, all he had to do was to get up and walk away.

When he reached the village he found that all his neighbors had been looking everywhere for him.

"That is," Grandaddy Beaver explained, "we looked everywhere except near the tree where you had that adventure a few nights ago. I said you wouldn't be there, for I advised you to keep away from that spot, as you will recall."

Now, Brownie Beaver said nothing more. He knew that it was an unheard-of thing for one of the Beaver family to be caught by a falling tree. To have everyone know what had happened to him would be a good deal like a disgrace.

But there are plenty of people who would think they had done something quite clever if they had gnawed through a tree with their teeth-- though that was something that never once entered Brownie Beaver's head.

XVIII
MR. FROG'S QUESTION

Why don't you get some new clothes?"

It was Mr. Frog that asked the question; and he asked it of Brownie Beaver, who was at work on top of his house. Mr. Frog had been hiding among the lily-pads, watching Brownie. But Brownie hadn't noticed him until he stuck his head out of the water and spoke.

At first Mr. Frog's question made Brownie a bit peevish.

"What's the matter with my clothes?" he asked hotly.

"There's nothing the matter with them--nothing at all," said Mr. Frog--"except that they are not as becoming to you as they might be. Of course," he added, as he saw that Brownie Beaver was frowning, "you look handsome in them. But you've no idea how you'd look in clothes of *my* making."

Brownie Beaver felt more agreeable as soon as Mr. Frog had told him what he meant.

"Do *you* make clothes?" he inquired.

"I'm a tailor," Mr. Frog replied. "And I've just opened a shop at the upper end of the pond."

"What's the matter with my tail?" Brownie snapped. He was angry again.

Then Mr. Frog explained that a tailor made suits.

"We've nothing to do with *tails,*" he said--"unless it's coat-tails."

"What about cattails?" Brownie asked. "You're pretty close to some right now. So you can hardly say you have nothing to do with them."

Mr. Frog smiled.

"I see you're a joker," he said. "And it really seems a pity," he went on, "that a bright young fellow like you shouldn't wear the finest clothes to be had anywhere.

If you'll come to my shop I'll make you a suit such as you never saw before in all your life."

"I'll come!" Brownie Beaver promised. "I'll be there at sunset."

And he went. Mr. Frog was waiting for him, with a broad smile on his face. Any smile of his just had to be broad, because he had such a wide mouth.

"Come right in!" Mr. Frog said. "I'll measure you at once." So Brownie Beaver stepped inside Mr. Frog's shop to be measured for his new suit.

It was all over in a few minutes. Mr. Frog scratched some figures on a flat stone. And then he went into the back room of his shop.

He stayed there a long time. And when he came into the front part again he found Brownie Beaver still there.

"What are you waiting for?" Mr. Frog asked. He seemed surprised that Brownie had not left.

"I'm waiting for my suit, of course," Brownie Beaver said.

"Oh! That won't be ready for three days," Mr. Frog told him. "I have to make it, you know."

Brownie thought that Mr. Frog must be a slow worker; and he told him as much.

But Mr. Frog did not agree with him.

"I'm very spry!" he claimed. "On the jump every minute!"

As Brownie started away, Mr. Frog called him back.

"I'd get a new hat if I were you," he suggested.

"What's the matter with this hat?" Brownie wanted to know. "It's a beaver hat--one my great-grandfather used to wear. It's been in our family a good many years and I'd hate to part with it."

"You needn't part with it," Mr. Frog said pleasantly. "Just don't wear it--that's all! For it won't look well with the clothes I'm going to make for you."

Then Brownie Beaver moved away once more. And again Mr. Frog stopped him.

"I'd buy a collar if I were you," he said.

"What's the matter with this neckerchief?" Brownie Beaver demanded. "It belonged to my great-grandmother."

"Then I'd be careful of it if I were you," Mr. Frog told him. "And please get a stiff white collar to wear."

"Won't it get limp in the water?" Brownie asked, doubtfully.

"Get a celluloid one, of course," Mr. Frog replied. "That's the only kind of collar you ought to wear."

So Brownie Beaver left the tailor-shop. And he was feeling quite unhappy. He had always been satisfied with his clothes. But now he began to dislike everything he had on. And he could hardly wait for three day to pass, he was in such a hurry for Mr. Frog to finish his new suit.

XIX
THE NEW SUIT

Three days had passed. And as soon as he had finished his breakfast Brownie Beaver hastened to the tailor-shop of Mr. Frog, who had been making him a suit of clothes.

Much to Brownie's disappointment, he found that Mr. Frog's door was locked. But he sat down on the doorstep and waited a long time. And at last Mr. Frog appeared.

After bidding Brownie Beaver good-morning, Mr. Frog yawned widely, remarking that he had been out late the night before, "at a singing-party," he said. "What can I do for you?" he asked Brownie Beaver.

"You can let me have my new suit of clothes," Brownie told him.

"You must be mistaken," Mr. Frog replied. "I don't remember you. I'm not making any suit for you."

At that Brownie Beaver became much excited.

"Why--" he exclaimed--"I was here three days ago and you measured me.... Don't you know me now?" he asked.

"Sorry to say I don't," was Mr. Frog's answer.

Brownie Beaver was desperate. He had looked forward eagerly to having his new suit. And he wanted it at once.

"You advised me to get a new hat and a collar," Brownie reminded him.

Mr. Frog smiled.

"Ah! That's it!" he cried. "You're wearing them now; and it's no wonder I didn't recognize you. You look ten years younger."

Brownie Beaver was puzzled.

"I'm not ten yet," he said. "So if I look ten years younger, I must appear very young indeed."

"The new clothes will fix that," Mr. Frog assured him.

"But you just told me you were not making a suit for me," said Brownie.

"Quite true, too!" answered Mr. Frog--"because it's all finished. So, of course, I'm not making it now."

They had stepped inside the shop. And Mr. Frog carefully took some garments off a peg and spread them before Brownie Beaver.

"There!" he said with an air of pride. "The finest suit you ever saw!"

"I'll slip it on," said Brownie.

"Oh! I wouldn't do that!" Mr. Frog told him. "You might stretch it."

But nothing could have kept Brownie Beaver out of his new suit. He scrambled into it quickly, while the tailor stood by with a worried look upon his face.

"The coat seems to be all right," Brownie remarked. "But there's something wrong with the trousers. I can't see my feet!" He bent over and gazed down where his feet ought to have been. But they had vanished. And an end of each trouser-leg trailed on the floor. "These trousers are too long!" Brownie declared.

"Then you stretched them, putting them on," Mr. Frog said. "I warned you, you know."

"I was very careful," Brownie said. "I'm sure it can't be that."

"Then your legs are too short," Mr. Frog told him glibly. "They look to me to be *much* shorter than they were when I measured you."

"My legs--" Brownie Beaver exclaimed--"my legs are exactly the same length they were three days ago! You've made a mistake, Mr. Frog. That's what's the matter with these trousers!"

But Mr. Frog shook his head.

"I made them according to your measurements," he insisted.

"Let me see your figures!" Brownie Beaver cried.

But Mr. Frog shook his head again.

"I don't do business that way," he explained. "As soon as I've finished a suit I throw away the stone on which I've written the measurements. It saves trouble, if there's any complaint afterwards."

"Well!" said Brownie. "What can we do about this? I can't wear the trousers as they are."

"You'll have to get your legs stretched," Mr. Frog told him. "Just tie a stone to each foot and wear the trousers for a few days. As soon as you see your feet, take off the stones.... It's simple enough." He helped tie some heavy stones to Brownie's feet. And then Brownie swam away.

Now, swimming with your feet weighted like that is no easy matter. But Brownie managed to reach home. He stayed there, too, for the rest of the day, because it was hard for him to move about. And since he had nothing else to do, he went to sleep.

When he awoke, about an hour before sunset, he couldn't think at first what made his feet feel so heavy. He thought he must be ill--until he remembered about the stones being tied to his feet.

Then he looked down. And to his great surprise and joy there were his feet sticking out of his trousers, just as they ought to stick out!

Brownie untied the stones. He had not supposed his legs would stretch so quickly as that. And he told himself that Mr. Frog was a good tailor. He certainly knew his business. Now, as a matter of fact, Mr. Frog was a very careless person. He had thrown away Brownie's measurements **before** he made his clothes, instead of **afterwards**. And he had made the new suit entirely by guesswork. It was only natural that he would make some mistake; and so he had cut the trousers entirely too long.

When he discovered that, he wanted to get Brownie out of his shop. And what happened next was simply this: After Brownie's trousers were wet in the pond, they dried while he was sleeping. And while they were drying they were shrinking at the same time.

Though Brownie Beaver didn't know it, his legs had not stretched at all. They were exactly the same length they had always been.

The Codes Of Hammurabi And Moses
W. W. Davies

QTY

The discovery of the Hammurabi Code is one of the greatest achievements of archaeology, and is of paramount interest, not only to the student of the Bible, but also to all those interested in ancient history...

Religion   **ISBN:** *1-59462-338-4*   **Pages:132**
MSRP $12.95

The Theory of Moral Sentiments
Adam Smith

QTY

This work from 1749. contains original theories of conscience amd moral judgment and it is the foundation for systemof morals.

Philosophy **ISBN:** *1-59462-777-0*   **Pages:536**
MSRP $19.95

Jessica's First Prayer
Hesba Stretton

QTY

In a screened and secluded corner of one of the many railway-bridges which span the streets of London there could be seen a few years ago, from five o'clock every morning until half past eight, a tidily set-out coffee-stall, consisting of a trestle and board, upon which stood two large tin cans, with a small fire of charcoal burning under each so as to keep the coffee boiling during the early hours of the morning when the work-people were thronging into the city on their way to their daily toil...

Pages:84

Childrens   **ISBN:** *1-59462-373-2*   *MSRP $9.95*

My Life and Work
Henry Ford

QTY

Henry Ford revolutionized the world with his implementation of mass production for the Model T automobile. Gain valuable business insight into his life and work with his own auto-biography... "We have only started on our development of our country we have not as yet, with all our talk of wonderful progress, done more than scratch the surface. The progress has been wonderful enough but..."

Pages:300

Biographies/   **ISBN:** *1-59462-198-5*   *MSRP $21.95*

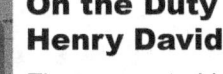

The Art of Cross-Examination
Francis Wellman

QTY

I presume it is the experience of every author, after his first book is published upon an important subject, to be almost overwhelmed with a wealth of ideas and illustrations which could readily have been included in his book, and which to his own mind, at least, seem to make a second edition inevitable. Such certainly was the case with me; and when the first edition had reached its sixth impression in five months, I rejoiced to learn that it seemed to my publishers that the book had met with a sufficiently favorable reception to justify a second and considerably enlarged edition. ..

Reference   **ISBN:** *1-59462-647-2*   **Pages:412**   *MSRP $19.95*

On the Duty of Civil Disobedience
Henry David Thoreau

QTY

Thoreau wrote his famous essay, On the Duty of Civil Disobedience, as a protest against an unjust but popular war and the immoral but popular institution of slave-owning. He did more than write—he declined to pay his taxes, and was hauled off to gaol in consequence. Who can say how much this refusal of his hastened the end of the war and of slavery ?

Law   **ISBN:** *1-59462-747-9*   **Pages:48**   **MSRP $7.45**

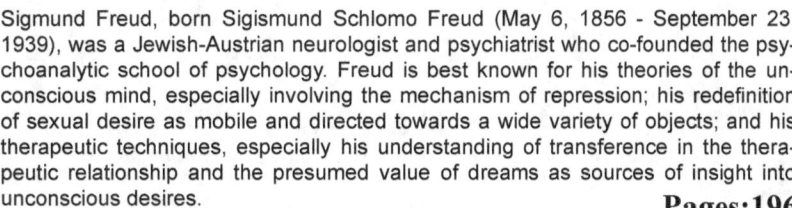

Dream Psychology Psychoanalysis for Beginners
Sigmund Freud

QTY

Sigmund Freud, born Sigismund Schlomo Freud (May 6, 1856 - September 23, 1939), was a Jewish-Austrian neurologist and psychiatrist who co-founded the psychoanalytic school of psychology. Freud is best known for his theories of the unconscious mind, especially involving the mechanism of repression; his redefinition of sexual desire as mobile and directed towards a wide variety of objects; and his therapeutic techniques, especially his understanding of transference in the therapeutic relationship and the presumed value of dreams as sources of insight into unconscious desires.

Psychology   **ISBN:** *1-59462-905-6*   **Pages:196**   *MSRP $15.45*

The Miracle of Right Thought
Orison Swett Marden

QTY

Believe with all of your heart that you will do what you were made to do. When the mind has once formed the habit of holding cheerful, happy, prosperous pictures, it will not be easy to form the opposite habit. It does not matter how improbable or how far away this realization may see, or how dark the prospects may be, if we visualize them as best we can, as vividly as possible, hold tenaciously to them and vigorously struggle to attain them, they will gradually become actualized, realized in the life. But a desire, a longing without endeavor, a yearning abandoned or held indifferently will vanish without realization.

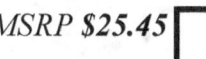

Self Help   **ISBN:** *1-59462-644-8*   **Pages:360**   *MSRP $25.45*

QTY

The Rosicrucian Cosmo-Conception Mystic Christianity *by Max Heindel*   ISBN: *1-59462-188-8*   **$38.95**
The Rosicrucian Cosmo-conception is not dogmatic, neither does it appeal to any other authority than the reason of the student. It is: not controversial, but is: sent forth in the, hope that it may help to clear...   New Age/Religion Pages 646

Abandonment To Divine Providence *by Jean-Pierre de Caussade*   ISBN: *1-59462-228-0*   **$25.95**
"The Rev. Jean Pierre de Caussade was one of the most remarkable spiritual writers of the Society of Jesus in France in the 18th Century. His death took place at Toulouse in 1751. His works have gone through many editions and have been republished...   Inspirational/Religion Pages 400

Mental Chemistry *by Charles Haanel*   ISBN: *1-59462-192-6*   **$23.95**
Mental Chemistry allows the change of material conditions by combining and appropriately utilizing the power of the mind. Much like applied chemistry creates something new and unique out of careful combinations of chemicals the mastery of mental chemistry...   New Age Pages 354

The Letters of Robert Browning and Elizabeth Barret Barrett 1845-1846 vol II   ISBN: *1-59462-193-4*   **$35.95**
by Robert Browning and Elizabeth Barrett   Biographies Pages 596

Gleanings In Genesis (volume I) *by Arthur W. Pink*   ISBN: *1-59462-130-6*   **$27.45**
Appropriately has Genesis been termed "the seed plot of the Bible" for in it we have, in germ form, almost all of the great doctrines which are afterwards fully developed in the books of Scripture which follow...   Religion/Inspirational Pages 420

The Master Key *by L. W. de Laurence*   ISBN: *1-59462-001-6*   **$30.95**
In no branch of human knowledge has there been a more lively increase of the spirit of research during the past few years than in the study of Psychology, Concentration and Mental Discipline. The requests for authentic lessons in Thought Control, Mental Discipline and...   New Age/Business Pages 422

The Lesser Key Of Solomon Goetia *by L. W. de Laurence*   ISBN: *1-59462-092-X*   **$9.95**
This translation of the first book of the "Lernegton" which is now for the first time made accessible to students of Talismanic Magic was done, after careful collation and edition, from numerous Ancient Manuscripts in Hebrew, Latin, and French...   New Age/Occult Pages 92

Rubaiyat Of Omar Khayyam *by Edward Fitzgerald*   ISBN:*1-59462-332-5*   **$13.95**
Edward Fitzgerald, whom the world has already learned, in spite of his own efforts to remain within the shadow of anonymity, to look upon as one of the rarest poets of the century, was born at Bredfield, in Suffolk, on the 31st of March, 1809. He was the third son of John Purcell...   Music Pages 172

Ancient Law *by Henry Maine*   ISBN: *1-59462-128-4*   **$29.95**
The chief object of the following pages is to indicate some of the earliest ideas of mankind, as they are reflected in Ancient Law, and to point out the relation of those ideas to modern thought.   Religion/History Pages 452

Far-Away Stories *by William J. Locke*   ISBN: *1-59462-129-2*   **$19.45**
"Good wine needs no bush, but a collection of mixed vintages does. And this book is just such a collection. Some of the stories I do not want to remain buried for ever in the museum files of dead magazine-numbers an author's not unpardonable vanity..."   Fiction Pages 272

Life of David Crockett *by David Crockett*   ISBN: *1-59462-250-7*   **$27.45**
"Colonel David Crockett was one of the most remarkable men of the times in which he lived. Born in humble life, but gifted with a strong will, an indomitable courage, and unremitting perseverance...   Biographies/New Age Pages 424

Lip-Reading *by Edward Nitchie*   ISBN: *1-59462-206-X*   **$25.95**
Edward B. Nitchie, founder of the New York School for the Hard of Hearing, now the Nitchie School of Lip-Reading, Inc, wrote "LIP-READING Principles and Practice". The development and perfecting of this meritorious work on lip-reading was an undertaking...   How-to Pages 400

A Handbook of Suggestive Therapeutics, Applied Hypnotism, Psychic Science   ISBN: *1-59462-214-0*   **$24.95**
by Henry Munro   Health/New Age/Health/Self-help Pages 376

A Doll's House: and Two Other Plays *by Henrik Ibsen*   ISBN: *1-59462-112-8*   **$19.95**
Henrik Ibsen created this classic when in revolutionary 1848 Rome. Introducing some striking concepts in playwriting for the realist genre, this play has been studied the world over.   Fiction/Classics/Plays 308

The Light of Asia *by sir Edwin Arnold*   ISBN: *1-59462-204-3*   **$13.95**
In this poetic masterpiece, Edwin Arnold describes the life and teachings of Buddha. The man who was to become known as Buddha to the world was born as Prince Gautama of India but he rejected the worldly riches and abandoned the reigns of power when...   Religion/History/Biographies Pages 170

The Complete Works of Guy de Maupassant *by Guy de Maupassant*   ISBN: *1-59462-157-8*   **$16.95**
"For days and days, nights and nights, I had dreamed of that first kiss which was to consecrate our engagement, and I knew not on what spot I should put my lips..."   Fiction/Classics Pages 240

The Art of Cross-Examination *by Francis L. Wellman*   ISBN: *1-59462-309-0*   **$26.95**
Written by a renowned trial lawyer, Wellman imparts his experience and uses case studies to explain how to use psychology to extract desired information through questioning.   How-to/Science/Reference Pages 408

Answered or Unanswered? *by Louisa Vaughan*   ISBN: *1-59462-248-5*   **$10.95**
Miracles of Faith in China   Religion Pages 112

The Edinburgh Lectures on Mental Science (1909) *by Thomas*   ISBN: *1-59462-008-3*   **$11.95**
This book contains the substance of a course of lectures recently given by the writer in the Queen Street Hall, Edinburgh. Its purpose is to indicate the Natural Principles governing the relation between Mental Action and Material Conditions...   New Age/Psychology Pages 148

Ayesha *by H. Rider Haggard*   ISBN: *1-59462-301-5*   **$24.95**
Verily and indeed it is the unexpected that happens! Probably if there was one person upon the earth from whom the Editor of this, and of a certain previous history, did not expect to hear again...   Classics Pages 380

Ayala's Angel *by Anthony Trollope*   ISBN: *1-59462-352-X*   **$29.95**
The two girls were both pretty, but Lucy who was twenty-one who supposed to be simple and comparatively unattractive, whereas Ayala was credited, as her Bombwhat romantic name might show, with poetic charm and a taste for romance. Ayala when her father died was nineteen...   Fiction Pages 484

The American Commonwealth *by James Bryce*   ISBN: *1-59462-286-8*   **$34.45**
An interpretation of American democratic political theory. It examines political mechanics and society from the perspective of Scotsman James Bryce   Politics Pages 572

Stories of the Pilgrims *by Margaret P. Pumphrey*   ISBN: *1-59462-116-0*   **$17.95**
This book explores pilgrims religious oppression in England as well as their escape to Holland and eventual crossing to America on the Mayflower, and their early days in New England...   History Pages 268

QTY

The Fasting Cure by *Sinclair Upton*   **ISBN:** *1-59462-222-1*   **$13.95**
In the Cosmopolitan Magazine for May, 1910, and in the Contemporary Review (London) for April, 1910, I published an article dealing with my experiences in fasting. I have written a great many magazine articles, but never one which attracted so much attention... New Age/Self Help/Health Pages 164

Hebrew Astrology by *Sepharial*   **ISBN:** *1-59462-308-2*   **$13.45**
In these days of advanced thinking it is a matter of common observation that we have left many of the old landmarks behind and that we are now pressing forward to greater heights and to a wider horizon than that which represented the mind-content of our progenitors...   Astrology Pages 144

Thought Vibration or The Law of Attraction in the Thought World   **ISBN:** *1-59462-127-6*   **$12.95**

by *William Walker Atkinson*   Psychology/Religion Pages 144

Optimism by *Helen Keller*   **ISBN:** *1-59462-108-X*   **$15.95**
Helen Keller was blind, deaf, and mute since 19 months old, yet famously learned how to overcome these handicaps, communicate with the world, and spread her lectures promoting optimism. An inspiring read for everyone...   Biographies/Inspirational Pages 84

Sara Crewe by *Frances Burnett*   **ISBN:** *1-59462-360-0*   **$9.45**
In the first place, Miss Minchin lived in London. Her home was a large, dull, tall one, in a large, dull square, where all the houses were alike, and all the sparrows were alike, and where all the door-knockers made the same heavy sound...   Childrens/Classic Pages 88

The Autobiography of Benjamin Franklin by *Benjamin Franklin*   **ISBN:** *1-59462-135-7*   **$24.95**
The Autobiography of Benjamin Franklin has probably been more extensively read than any other American historical work, and no other book of its kind has had such ups and downs of fortune. Franklin lived for many years in England, where he was agent...   Biographies/History Pages 332

Name	
Email	
Telephone	
Address	
City, State ZIP	

☐ **Credit Card**   ☐ **Check / Money Order**

Credit Card Number	
Expiration Date	
Signature	

Please Mail to: Book Jungle
                     PO Box 2226
                     Champaign, IL 61825
or Fax to: 630-214-0564

ORDERING INFORMATION

web*: www.bookjungle.com*
email*: sales@bookjungle.com*
fax*: 630-214-0564*
mail*: Book Jungle PO Box 2226 Champaign, IL 61825*
or PayPal *to sales@bookjungle.com*

Please contact us for bulk discounts

DIRECT-ORDER TERMS

**20% Discount if You Order
Two or More Books**
Free Domestic Shipping!
Accepted: Master Card, Visa,
Discover, American Express